This series of books empowers children to realize that regardless of their age, they can make a difference through kindness and good deeds. The stories will inspire them to rely on God to provide guidance and direction, as they seek to help others.

This is Aiden. He lives here with his mom, dad, and his grandmother. He calls his grandmother MiMa.

MiMa had gotten sick, so she moved into their house. Aiden knew that sometimes it was hard for his mom and dad to take care of her, but he knew how much MiMa appreciated their help.

Meet Aiden's best friends…Jaden, Andrew, and Lily.

Every morning they picked Aiden up and gave him a ride to school. He would ride on the back of Jaden's bike.

Each day on their way to school, they passed the bike store where Aiden saw the shiniest and coolest bike he had ever seen!

Aiden was very grateful for his friends and that they gave him a ride, but he REALLY wished he had a bike of his own.

Aiden's mom did not work because she stayed home to take care of MiMa. His parents could not afford to buy him his own bike right now.

Aiden's friends felt sorry for him.

They wanted so badly to help him get his own bike. How could they help him, they wondered???

Lily said they should pray and ask God to show them how they can help Aiden. That is just what they did. They prayed for God to show them what they should do…and He did.

Suddenly Jaden had an idea!

They went to their parents and asked if they could do extra chores to make money.

On the weekends, they mowed the grass at their houses

Their moms helped them make cookies and lemonade. Jaden's dad built them a stand where they could sell their goodies. They decorated it with banners and signs and made it the most FUN lemonade stand they had ever seen. They were so proud of their stand, and especially happy that they sold all of their cookies and lemonade!

They went to their neighbors. Can you hire us to walk your dogs? We will take good care of them!

The neighbors agreed and were excited that the children were going to help them with their dogs. Lily really loved this job. Even though it was a job, she had so much fun and knew it was going to help them reach their goal to buy Aiden a bike. Their furry four-legged friends were especially happy to go for walks.

FINALLY, after four weeks of hard work, they had enough money to buy the bike for Aiden!

Yay!, they said as they jumped up and down, and high-fived each other. We did it!, they cheered. Then they thanked God for giving them such a great idea and helping them accomplish their plan.

The next morning, they picked up Aiden, but this time when they saw the bike shop, they stopped. They went inside and bought the bike for Aiden.

They came out of the store and yelled, "SURPRISE!"
Then they gave the bike to Aiden.

Aiden hugged his friends. He could not believe it! He thought, you are just kids like me...how did you do such a kind and special thing for me?

They explained to Aiden, We weren't sure we could do it at first, but we prayed and asked God to help us. And He did! He showed us that just because we are kids, doesn't mean we can't find a way to help people. He gave us the idea for our great plan, and then gave us the confidence to succeed!

Aiden was so grateful for what his friends had done for him. Now, he understood what they had told him.. If he wants to do something to help others, he just has to believe in himself and rely on God's help to show him the best way.

He made a promise that he was going to pray to find someone else who had a need, and he was going to help fill that need!

You can do the same thing. Ask God how He can help you fill the needs of others by doing kind things. Rely on Him and you will do amazing things!

I can do all things through Christ who strengthens me

Philippians 4:13

GOOD DEEDS FILL NEEDS!